. . . and pretend that I'm a fairy princess in a very important ballet.
When the show's over, the audience will throw so many flowers on
stage that my dressing room will look like a flower shop.

In the winter I pretend that I'm on the beach in the Riviera—that's in France.

PAGES 2-3

PAGES 4-5

PAGES 6-7

PAGES 8-9

PAGES IO-II

PAGES 6-7

SUN TAN

Nanny says the salt air is good for my complexion,
but that I mustn't get too much sun sun sun.

I love to explore, so often we set off for the jungle where we meet some very nice monkeys. I want to take one home with me, but Nanny says no no no.

The Plaza already has one monkey. She means me—ELOISE!

Most of all I like to pretend I'm a model
for a famous fashion designer who will plan
his entire fall collection around me.
Ooooooooooo, I absolutely love to dress up!